DETECTIVE Zack

Danger at Dinosaur Camp

D0032914

Written by
Jerry D. Thomas

Illustrated by
Lad Odell

Equipping Kids for Life!
faithkids.com

A Faith Building Guide can be found on page 126.

Faith Building Guide

Ages 9 and up

Courage

Faith Kids® is an imprint of
Cook Communications Ministries, Colorado Springs, CO 80918
Cook Communications, Paris, Ontario
Kingsway Communications, Eastbourne, England

DETECTIVE ZACK: DANGER AT DINOSAUR CAMP
© 2002 by Jerry D. Thomas

All rights reserved. No part of this book may be reproduced without written
permission, except for brief quotations in books and critical reviews. For
information, write Cook Communications Ministries, 4050 Lee Vance View,
Colorado Springs, CO 80918.

First Printing, 1992 (Pacific Press)
First Faith Kids® Printing, 2002
Printed in the United States of America
1 2 3 4 5 6 7 8 9 10 Printing/Year 06 05 04 03 02

Edited by: Phyllis Williams
Designed by: Big Mouth Bass Design, Inc.
Cover Illustrated by: Lad Odell

Unless otherwise noted, Scripture quotations are taken from the *HOLY
BIBLE: NEW INTERNATIONAL VERSION*®. Copyright © 1973, 1978, 1984
by International Bible Society. Used by permission of Zondervan Publishing
House. All rights reserved.

Library of Congress Cataloging-in-Publication Data

Thomas, Jerry D., 1959-
    [Detective Zack: danger at Dinosaur Camp]
    Detective Zack: danger at Dinosaur Camp / written by Jerry D. Thomas.
    p. cm.
    Summary: While Zack and his family attend Dinosaur Camp to try to rec-
oncile the Bible's creation story with scientific knowledge about dinosaurs,
they become involved in some current detective work as well.
    ISBN0-7814-3732-6
    [1. Dinosaurs--Fiction. 2. Christian life--Fiction. 3. Paleontology--Fiction.
4. Mystery and detective stories.] I. Title.

PZ7.T366954 Dan 2002
[Fic]--dc21   2001033206

Dedication

To those who knew me
before I was "anybody" in writing,
and whose encouragement helped change that:

Aileen Andres Sox
(who published my first children's story),
Chris Blake,
Barbara Coffen,
Kermit Netteburg,
Cec Murphey,
Elaine Grove,
and my brother, David.

At least now, everyone will know who to blame.

Books in this Series

(1)   Detective Zack: Secret of Noah's Flood

(2)   Detective Zack: Mystery at Thunder Mountain

(3)   Detective Zack: Danger at Dinosaur Camp

(4)   Detective Zack: Secrets in the Sand

(5)   Detective Zack: Red Hat Mystery

(6)   Detective Zack: Missing Manger Mystery

Contents

1   Back to the Tent   7

2   Dinosaur Camp   15

3   Clues in the Canyon   23

4   Trouble!   31

5   Outlaw Trap   41

6   Footprints in the Canyon   51

7   Dinosaurs on the Ceiling   59

8   Strange Stones, Strange Moans   69

9   Dinosaur Roar?   79

10   A Story in the Sand   87

11   White-Water Danger   97

12   Batteries Not Included   107

13   Dino-Surprise!   115

14   Some of God's Favorites   121

Faith Building Guide   126

ONE

Back to the Tent

A Mystery Already

It's hard to write by campfire light. *Ow!* Especially when mosquitos are treating you like a pincushion. I was writing in my tent, but one mosquito had snuck inside. I tracked it down and smashed it—with my flashlight. Now, of course, my flashlight doesn't work.

Did mosquitos really bite dinosaurs? I'll have to ask Professor Bones.

Ow! If there were this many mosquitos when the dinosaurs lived here, no wonder the dinosaurs all died. They probably ran out of blood.

Except for the mosquitos, I like this campground. The canyon wall goes almost straight up on one side and the river is so close I can hear it all the time. Except for the river, it's very quiet here. Not like it was this afternoon when we arrived.

People were shouting, dust was flying, the lights on the sheriff's car were flashing—it was fun to watch!

"Our radio was stolen," a man beside a brown travel trailer was saying. "It was an expensive one, too. Ranger, I expect you to find it."

A woman in a park ranger uniform held up her hand. "I'm sorry, Sheriff Tate," she said. "I hate to drag you all the way out here, but it seems like we have some kind of thief in the camp."

"I was already out here anyway, Ranger Mahoney. Now, most likely, whoever took it is right here in this campground. So if someone here, like one of you kids, has done something they already regret, how about just returning it and let's all get on with our vacations."

The sheriff turned slowly and looked at each of the kids standing around. When he got to my sister and me, I raised my hands. "Hey, don't look at me. I just got here."

Sheriff Tate raised an eyebrow and almost smiled. Then he cleared his throat. "Folks, keep an eye on your kids. Ranger Mahoney, let's talk down at the ranger station."

"What's going on?" my sister Kayla asked a kid standing nearby. I found out later that his name is Luis.

He shrugged. "My family just got here a few hours ago. All I know is, two or three people claimed things have been stolen from their tents or campers."

"Is anything missing from your camp?" I asked.

Luis shook his head. "I'm afraid the ranger might

think I'm the thief, because stuff started disappearing right after we got here."

I thought about that. "Did it disappear then, or is that just when people noticed it was gone?"

Snap! He snapped his fingers. "Hey, that's right. Both of those people were gone on a hike all morning. They got back about the time we arrived. And that's when they noticed that things were missing."

"So the thief could have stolen those things any time while they were gone," I finished. "See, I knew you didn't do it."

"Thanks," Luis said. "Now all I have to do is convince the ranger." He pointed across the way to another campsite. "I think they did it."

Kayla and I stared at the campsite.

Luis went on. "Those tents are filled with loud annoying teenagers. I've already heard them shouting at each other from here. And the ranger had to tell them to turn their music down this afternoon."

While we were watching, a boy with wild black hair crawled out of his tent with earphones on and bopped his way toward the river. Kayla shook her head. "Why do people do that? Why do they drive all the way out into the wilderness, and then listen to the same thing they hear at home?"

I had to agree with Luis. The teenagers were at the top of the suspect list.

"You kids going white water rafting?" A man held some papers out in front of the red raft badge on his shirt. The name "Buddy" was sewn on the other side. He said, "Be sure you take a Red Raft River trip while you're here. Don't miss the chance to ride the Warm Springs Rapids."

"Thanks," I said as we all took one. "We're going on a raft ride sometime this week."

"Hope it's with us," Buddy said as he walked away.

"I'm supposed to go rafting too," Luis said. It turned out that Luis's family is here for the same reason mine is. Their red and blue tents are only a few spaces away from ours.

So why am I fighting mosquitos in Dinosaur Land? It's a long story. Since the wind is blowing the campfire smoke right at me, I'll hold my breath and write as fast as I can. (Hey, at least the smoke keeps the mosquitos away!)

This year at school, it seems like everyone was talking about dinosaurs. So was I—I like dinosaurs. I think the tyrannosaurus rex was amazing. But my favorite is the brachiosaurs. They were so big, and with those long necks, they stuck their heads up out of the trees like a submarine sticks up a periscope.

Bobby and I and Scott, a kid who just moved to our

neighborhood, played dinosaurs out in the woods a lot. But every time we talked about dinosaurs, there was an argument.

"I wish I had lived back when the dinosaurs were around," I said one day.

"Ha!" Scott laughed. "That's crazy. Everyone knows that dinosaurs lived millions of years before there were any people."

"I'm just wishing," I answered. "Besides, the Bible says that God created everything in six days. So people and dinosaurs must have been alive at the same time."

"Look," Scott said, "scientists can prove that dinosaurs lived millions of years before there were any people."

I knew that the correct word for a scientist who studies bones and fossils is *paleontologist* (pay-lee-on-tall-o-gist). But I didn't say anything.

Scott went on. "So the Bible can't be right. But who cares—let's play before I have to go."

Well I cared. And after Scott left, I found out that Bobby cared too. "Zack, do you think Scott was right about dinosaurs? Do you think the Bible is wrong?"

Bobby used to think that the Bible stories were fairy tales and that scientists could prove it. But after I showed him scientific evidence that supports the story of Noah's flood, he decided that maybe the Bible is true.

I shrugged. "I believe the Bible is true, but I don't think it says anything about dinosaurs. I don't really know how paleontologists who believe in the Bible explain dinosaurs. I wish I knew how to find out."

"Yeah," Bobby agreed, "there aren't any dinosaurs around now to study. And how much can you learn from a bunch of bones and fossils? I guess we'll never really know."

I thought Bobby was right about dinosaurs. It turns out we might both be wrong.

Ow! As soon as the smoke cleared enough to breathe, another mosquito bit me. I still haven't explained about where we are or why I'm writing in my notebook this time, but it'll have to wait. I'm heading back to the tent.

Discoveries and Clues

Dinosaur Clues

If dinosaurs really lived millions of years ago, how can the Bible story of creation be true?

If the Bible story is true, then dinosaurs and people lived at the same time.

Words to Remember

Paleontologist: A scientist who studies bones and fossils to learn about animals or plants that lived long ago

Dinosaur Camp

A Herd of What!?

Something woke me up out of a deep sleep. I peeked through my eyelashes enough to see that it was barely light. When I didn't hear anything but the river, I almost fell back asleep.

Then I heard it again. Someone was screaming. And getting closer. That time, I sat up and reached for the tent flap zipper.

"What's going on?" Kayla asked as I brushed past her.

"I don't know. If I could get this zipper to move we might find out." She pulled the other way and finally the flap zipped open. We both stuck our heads out far enough to see a small crowd of badly-dressed people with wild hair.

"I saw it up there!" a woman was half-shouting. She pointed toward a canyon that wound its way back up toward the top of the *plateau* (a flat-topped mountain).

"What?" someone asked, trying to calm her down, "you saw what?"

"I was nearly at the top, and the first rays of sunshine were hitting the canyon wall. I heard a strange noise, like something big shuffling over the rocks. Then I saw it. It had a long neck, like a tree trunk and a small head. Its jaws were snapping open and shut."

"She must have been sleepwalking," Kayla muttered.

Her friend tried to calm her again. "Are you sure? Maybe it was just a tree moving in the wind."

"Did you actually see it?" someone else asked.

"Not really," the woman admitted. "I just saw its shadow against the canyon wall. But then it started chasing me! I heard pounding footsteps above me. It sounded like a whole herd of them! So I ran."

Everyone just stood there for a minute. Finally, someone asked the question I had. "A whole herd of what?"

The woman covered her face. "You're going to think I'm crazy, but it was—a dinosaur!"

Most people tried to hide their smiles. Not Kayla. She laughed out loud. "Ha! Now I know she was still asleep. And dreaming!"

"I'm not crazy," the woman said to her friends. "It was one of those dinosaurs with the long necks."

"OK," her friend said. "Let's just go make some breakfast."

"I'm going to pack!" the woman said. "My family's

not staying here a minute longer. Not with a whole herd of killer dinosaurs running around loose."

After that, everyone else walked away. Kayla and I stretched back out in our sleeping bags. "What do you think she saw?" I asked.

"Who knows? The sun must have been shining right in her eyes or something. There's no way any dinosaurs are wandering around out there. Is there?"

Luis had the same question when we saw him later. "That woman must have been *loco en la cabesa*," Luis said.

Kayla and I stared at him. "What?"

Luis grinned. "Loco. It's Spanish for crazy. She must have been crazy in the head. There are no real dinosaurs around here, right?"

"Wrong."

We all whirled around to see who was talking. It was Ranger Mahoney, walking up on a horse. "Hundreds of real dinosaurs have been found around here," she said. "Real dinosaur fossils, that is. These dinosaurs are real, but they've been dead a long time. Fifty or sixty million years, most scientists think."

"Ranger Mahoney," Kayla asked, "what do you think that woman saw this morning?"

The ranger smiled. "Like I've been telling people all morning, there are no living dinosaurs here or anywhere else on earth. We have bobcats, coyotes, sometimes even wolves and mountain lions, but no dinosaurs. I don't know what she saw, but she must have been confused by the early morning light."

"No one else has ever reported seeing a thing like that?" I asked.

She shrugged. "People have been seeing strange things out here ever since this land became a national park. I think people want it to be spooky because of all the dinosaur bones. I think they enjoy a good scare. But we haven't lost any kids to the dinosaurs yet—and we're not going to this summer. You guys have a fun day."

She walked her horse toward another campsite, probably to answer the same questions.

"See, I knew I was right," Kayla said.

"I heard what she said," I agreed. "Did you hear what she didn't say?"

Kayla put her hands on her hips. "How could we hear something if she didn't say it?"

"Yeah," Luis agreed. "What are you talking about?"

I raised my hands. "I asked her if anyone else had ever reported seeing something like the woman did this morning. Ranger Mahoney didn't say no."

They both thought about it. "But she … " Kayla started, then stopped.

"She said that people have seen a lot of strange things," Luis remembered.

"I think we should make plans to explore that canyon," I told them. "And soon, before anything erases whatever tracks there are."

Luis agreed to meet us right after lunch.

While I was pumping water to cook lunch in, I remembered the other thing Ranger Mahoney had said that I didn't like. She said that the dinosaurs had been dead for fifty or sixty million years.

She reminded me of Scott back home.

I need to finish explaining what we're doing here. After Bobby and I talked about the dinosaurs and the Bible, I waited until supper to spring it on my mom and dad.

I waited until Dad had just taken a big bite of mashed potatoes. "Why does the Bible lie about dinosaurs?" I asked. He nearly choked. Mom almost dropped her fork.

"Well, I guess it doesn't really lie," I said quickly, before they could answer. "It just doesn't say anything at all. Why doesn't God tell us about dinosaurs?"

Dad finally swallowed. "Well, Zack, that's a good question. Especially since the Bible teaches that the world was created only a few thousand years ago. We found out a little about dinosaurs the last time we went camping, but not much."

"I thought all the dinosaurs died in Noah's flood," my little brother Alex said.

"That's what I thought too," I said. "But Scott laughed at that. He says that scientists can prove that dinosaurs lived millions of years before there were any people. Can scientists prove that?"

Dad took another bite while Mom answered. "Bobby thought scientists could prove that the Flood never happened. We found out different. I think we could find out the same thing again."

I pointed my fork at her. "But how could we find out? Where could we go? It's not like we can go to the dinosaur zoo and see for ourselves."

"Hey, I want to go to the dinosaur zoo," Alex said. "Can we, Mom? Can we?"

Kayla rolled her eyes. "Alex, there's no such place. The dinosaurs are all dead."

"So, they could still be in a zoo. Just in a dead zoo," he argued.

"Alex is right," I interrupted them to say. "There are dinosaurs in dead zoos. They're called museums."

Alex stuck his tongue out at Kayla. "See, we can too go. Can't we, Mom?"

Mom sighed. "No, Alex. If you're going to argue with your sister, I'm not taking you anywhere."

"Sorry," he mumbled.

Dad cleared his throat. "I'll see what I can find out about dinosaurs, Zack. Maybe there's a book we can read or something."

A few weeks later, Dad had an announcement. "Well, Zack, I found out how to discover information about dinosaurs and the Bible."

"A new video or book?" I guessed.

"No, not a video. We're going to camp."

"Camp?" I thought about Thunder Mountain Camp. "That's great. But are all of us going?"

Dad laughed. "It's not summer camp. It's Dinosaur Camp."

"Dinosaur Camp!" Alex shouted. "Will dinosaurs be camping with us?"

Of course we told him they wouldn't. But now I'm not so sure.

THREE

Clues in the Canyon

Exploring on Our Own

Dinosaur Camp isn't like a summer camp for kids. It's really a summer school class for teachers and other adults who want to learn more about dinosaurs. This time it was being held at Dinosaur National Monument in Colorado.

Seven families, including Luis and his family, were there for Dinosaur Camp. The first meeting was at lunch. We gathered together at one set of picnic tables and a white-haired man stood up to speak.

"Welcome to Dinosaur Camp," he said. "I am Professor Boniol." He smiled at me and Luis and Kayla in the front row. "My friends call me Professor Bones."

"Great name for a dinosaur guy," Kayla whispered.

Professor Bones went on. "This week, we will be exploring evidence that dinosaurs really did live on this earth. And we'll see how the dinosaurs might have fit into the Bible's story of creation."

I got out my notebook.

"First," Professor Bones said, "a few words about our campground. Back in 1909, a paleontologist found eight pieces of an apatosaurus's backbone near here. The bones were stuck in a giant slab of sandstone. It was solid rock then, but at one point in the past, it must have been an enormous sandbar in a mighty river."

"Did he ever find the rest of the apatosaurus?" someone asked.

"He found more than one," Professor Bones answered. "Those dinosaur bones, piled up and covered over with silt by the river, became one of the biggest dinosaur finds in history. Since then, more than 350 tons of dinosaur bones have been dug out of that rock layer."

"Wow," Luis said. "That had to come from a lot of animals, even if they are dinosaurs. Professor Bones, were all the bones from apatosauruses?"

"No, more than fourteen different kinds of dinosaurs have been found here. You'll be able to see which kinds when we go to the Dinosaur Gardens. And you'll be able to see paleontologists at work when we visit the Quarry Visitor Center."

"Will we be able to dig up some dinosaur bones, too?" Kayla asked.

Professor Bones shook his head. "No, the only place where dinosaur bones are found around here is in the quarry itself. There are places in Montana or in Alberta, Canada where we could search for fossils and bones ourselves. But here in Dinosaur National Park, we'll have to settle for watching others dig."

"Awww," we all moaned.

"Don't worry," he said. "We'll be rafting down the river, exploring canyons and caves, and searching for Indian paintings on the stone walls. We'll be having all kinds of fun."

We agreed to go to the quarry later that afternoon. When the meeting was over, we ran after Professor Bones.

"Professor Bones," I said, "my name is Zack. Kayla and Luis and I are trying to find out as much as we can about dinosaurs and how they lived. Can you tell us more?"

He smiled at us. "What do you want, extra credit? Don't worry, you don't have to take a test at the end of the week."

Kayla stomped her foot. "You're teasing us! We know there's not a test. We just want to know more."

"Yes, yes," he answered, "my apologies. I should have known you were the curious types. Okay, what do you want to know?"

"Since you already mentioned the apatosaurus," I suggested, "tell us about that one."

Professor Bones sat back down at the picnic table. "May I borrow your notebook?" he asked me. I handed it over. What could be better than him writing in it?

He took a pencil out of his pocket and opened the notebook to a blank page. "What we call the apatosaurus, looked like this," he said, sketching as he talked. "They're closely related to the brachiosaurus. They have the big stocky body and long, long necks."

I thought about that strange woman's dinosaur. "Where would it live? In a place like this?" I pointed to the cliffs and shrubs.

"No, no. The brachiosaur would live near water, possibly in water part of the time. With their long necks, they could reach the tallest trees or farthest branches.

"The nostrils of their nose were on the top side of their heads—like some frogs. This made it possible to breathe with only the tips of their noses sticking out of the water. At least, some of them could. Others were so big, it seems impossible that they could have even breathed if their bodies were under water."

"How big were they?" Luis asked.

Professor Bones frowned. "It's hard to know for certain. But over where the Dinosaur Gardens are, there is a steel skeleton of a diplodocus (dye-plod-ick-uss), another relative of the brachiosaur. The skeleton there was based on bones dug up out here. It's seventy-six feet long and twenty-one feet high."

"Whoa," Kayla breathed. "And it could swim?"

"The diplodocus did, we think," Professor Bones added. "It was lighter than the others, and it probably stayed under water most of the time to hide from its enemies." He hopped up. "Sorry, but I have to go now. We'll talk again at the quarry."

"We need to get started on a trip of our own," I said after he left. "We should have just enough time to explore the canyon before our trip to the quarry."

Kayla ran to get our backpacks. "We're going exploring, Mom," she shouted to the tent. "We'll be back soon."

"Stay away from the river," the tent shouted back. "And be careful!"

After Luis got permission, we started up the canyon trail. It wasn't too hard to follow. "Either a lot of people walk up here every year," Kayla said, "or a lot of animals do."

"It's probably a deer trail," Luis said. "My dad says they like to follow the same paths to water every day. After long enough, it leaves a trail."

As we neared the top of the canyon, I bent down and

looked carefully at the ground. Putting out my arm, I stopped Kayla from going by.

"What are you doing?" she asked.

"I'm looking for tracks," I said. "And I don't want you to walk on them. If something was here this morning, it might have left tracks."

Luis laughed. "Would you know dinosaur tracks if you saw them? You don't see them every day."

"I've seen dino tracks," I said. "Remember those fossil tracks we saw in Texas, Kayla?"

"That's right, we did see tracks," she agreed. Then she shuddered. "If we find tracks that big, I'm packing up and leaving."

Just then, we heard a kind of scraping, shuffling sound. It was coming from somewhere in the rocks above us.

— FOUR —

Trouble!

Suspicion and Suspects

What is it?" hissed Kayla.

Luis and I backed up against the canyon wall. I waved Kayla over to us then stood still and listened.

"It came from up there," Luis whispered. He pointed up. The plateau at the top was only about ten feet over our heads.

"Isn't this where that woman said she saw it?" Kayla whispered. "Didn't she say she heard a scraping sound?"

Just then, something hit me on the head and bounced off. It was a pebble. Then pebbles started falling like rain. "Hey, let's get out of here!" I shouted.

We ran back down the canyon path like a real dinosaur was chasing us. But when we thundered into camp, no one would listen to our story.

They were already shouting about something else.

"Ranger, someone stole our walkie-talkies," a man in a blue baseball cap shouted. "We need those on our hikes."

"Where were they?" Ranger Mahoney asked. The man pointed in his truck's open window.

"They were right there on the floor beside those binoculars," the man stated.

"Was the window open?" the ranger asked.

The man nodded unhappily. "We were only gone for a minute. You'd think you could trust people for that long."

"You'd like to think so, but I guess you can't." Ranger Mahoney raised her voice so everyone around could hear. "People, please keep your things inside your vehicles with the doors locked until we figure out what's happening."

Professor Bones came up beside us. "Not another thing stolen, I hope."

"I'm afraid so," I said. "A pair of walkie-talkies this time." I glanced over at Luis and Kayla. "Professor, what would a dinosaur track look like?"

Before he could answer, someone else butted in. "Oh, there you are, Professor. I've been looking for you." It was Buddy from the raft company. "We need to go over your group's rafting plans. Is now a good time?"

Professor Bones looked at us. I waved him away. "We'll talk to you later," I said, "at the dinosaur quarry."

They left to talk about rafting and we started talking about the canyon.

"Hey, where were you kids when those walkie-talkies were stolen?" It was one of the campers.

"We were exploring that canyon," Luis explained as he pointed.

The man nodded his head. "I saw you running back down like someone was chasing you. What did you do—hide the stolen things and then run back before anyone missed you?"

"No," I said firmly. "We were ... just running. We didn't take anything."

What was I going to say? We thought a dinosaur was chasing us?

The camper stomped away. "I know he didn't believe us," Kayla moaned. "What can we do to prove we didn't steal anything?"

"Find out who did," I said. "Where are those teenagers?" We wandered slowly by their campsite. It was empty.

"Should we search their tent?" Kayla hissed.

"Imagine how it would look if someone saw us in their tent," I reminded her. "No, we'll have to catch them a different way."

"Not one of your traps," she moaned.

"Traps?" Luis asked.

"It's a long story," Kayla told him. "Let's just say that

Zack's traps almost always catch someone. And it's almost always the wrong person."

"Hey, Kayla, Zack," Mom called from across the campground. "Come on, it's time to go to the quarry."

A *quarry* is really just the hole left when people dig stuff out of the ground. But this quarry was special.

"The early dinosaur hunters shipped tons of bones from this hole," Professor Bones explained to the group. He led the way into a large building. "Fossils are still being dug up and studied here. But now we can watch it happen."

"Why does this building have windows on the inside?" Alex asked.

Luis and I rushed over to find out. "Look at those bones," Luis said, looking through the glass. "And those guys are digging up another one."

"That's right," the professor said. "This building was built around the quarry so that people could watch diggers at work. The glass windows let us see the paleontologists as they uncover dinosaur fossil bones. As you can see, they leave the bones in place so we can see them."

"Why is all the scaffolding stuff out there?" Kayla asked. "It looks like a construction site."

"Remember that fossils and fossil bones are very fragile," Professor Bones said. "Diggers are very careful not to disturb the bones. The scaffolding lets them work in the fossil area without walking on the bones. They don't want to break them or move them from the position they were found in."

"That's what archeologists do too," I said. "When they dig up an old city, it's very important to know exactly where a clay pot or a brick was found."

The professor nodded. "When they dig, they're getting clues from where they find objects. It helps them figure out when the people lived who used those things. For paleontologists, the position of the dinosaur bones sometimes helps us learn more about what the dinosaurs looked like or how they behaved."

"Why are those people painting the dirt?" Luis asked. He pointed to where two workers brushed at the dirt with little brushes.

"They're not painting. That's the safest way to move the dirt and dust away from the fossil bones," Professor Bones said.

"Hmmf," Mom said from behind us. "I think I'd rather use a vacuum cleaner."

I was curious about the dinosaur bones. "Professor, what do those bones down there tell us about the dinosaurs who lived here?"

Professor Bones scratched his head. "Well, Zack, the

bones here tell us something interesting. In some places, like in Wyoming, in Alberta, Canada, and in Montana, paleontologists have found complete skeletons with the bones basically in place, like they were when the dinosaur was alive."

"Is that how they could tell what the dinosaurs looked like?" Luis asked.

"Yes," Professor Bones answered. "Other clues tell us more about how they lived. The shape tells us that some dinosaurs, like the stegosaurus, moved like a lizard. Others, like the gallimymus or the velociraptors moved like birds."

"You mean they could fly?" Alex asked.

"No, they moved like a big bird that doesn't fly—like ostriches or emus. They probably ran like birds and lived in flocks or herds like some birds do."

"I like emus," Alex said. "Our Uncle Clint grows emus."

"He means that our uncle has an emu ranch," I explained. "He raises and sells them. We stopped there on our way here this summer."

Thanks to Alex, my question still wasn't answered. "What do those bones tell us?" I asked again, pointing down into the quarry.

"These bones tell us something important," Professor Bones said, "something that has to do with the Bible. There was an enormous collection of dinosaur bones here. But the reason diggers haven't found whole skeletons here is that most of them are all jumbled up together."

"You mean like someone had piled them here on purpose?" Kayla asked.

"You mean like they all came here to die, like a graveyard?" Luis asked.

Professor Bones smiled. "Most paleontologists, even those who think that these dinosaurs lived sixty-five million years ago, believed that these dinosaurs died in a *flash flood*."

I thought about the size of some of the dinosaurs. "That must have been a big flood," I said.

Professor Bones nodded. "Really big. It's quite likely that these dinosaurs didn't live around this area at all. The flood carried their drowned bodies here."

"It had to be Noah's flood," Kayla said. "Dinosaurs must have been alive when the Flood came—when Noah was alive."

Just then, someone behind us screamed. "My camera! It's been stolen!"

Discoveries and Clues

Dinosaur Clues

The position of the dinosaur bones sometimes helps us learn more about what the dinosaurs looked like or how they behaved.

Paleontologists believe that floods left the dinosaurs' bones in this quarry all jumbled up. It would take a big flood to move those drowned dinosaurs, so it could have been Noah's flood.

Words to Remember

Quarry: A big hole in the ground where something was dug out

Flash flood: A flood that happens quickly

Dinosaur Camp Mystery

Something or someone is up in that canyon. It can't be a living dinosaur—can it?

Someone has stolen a radio, a pair of walkie-talkies, and now maybe a camera.

FIVE

Outlaw Trap

Trying to Catch a Thief

I watched while people rushed over to the woman. She wasn't from our camp. A park security guard started asking questions.

"Did you see someone take it?"

"No," the woman answered. "I keep my camera right here in my bag, next to my wallet. When I reached for it to take a picture, it was gone."

"Did you have it here in the Quarry Visitor Center?" the guard asked, taking out a notepad.

The woman thought. "Well, I know I had it yesterday when we went rafting because I took pictures on the river. The bag's been with me ever since then. Except when I kept it in my car."

"Do you keep your car locked?" the guard asked. His pencil paused over the paper.

"Always," the woman answered.

The guard snapped his pad closed. "Unless you think

the camera was taken since you arrived here, there's not much I can do right now. If you'll come to the office, we'll write up a report and alert the other rangers. Have you seen any suspicious characters?" he asked as they walked away.

Professor Bones went on with his lecture to the adults who were there to learn about dinosaurs. Kayla and Luis and I stayed back by the water fountain.

"It must have been those teenagers," Kayla hissed as she bent down to drink.

I shook my head. "Probably someone else is saying it must have been us. We'd better find out who the thief is."

Luis was getting a drink next. He shook his head and water went everywhere. "Hey," Kayla said, "watch out."

"Sorry," Luis said. "Maybe we should just stay out of it. We don't want to make people think we have anything to do with the stealing."

"Don't worry," I told him. "I'm already working on a plan."

Now Kayla shook her head. "Worry."

We caught up with the others and listened to the rest of Professor Bones's talk. I got to ride back to camp with him, so I asked some more questions.

"Professor, does the Bible really say anything about dinosaurs?"

He thought for a second. "Maybe," he answered. "But

let's start at the beginning. Many scientists believe that life on earth evolved over millions and millions of years. Some believe that God started the process of evolution—some don't believe in God at all."

I nodded. "But we believe that God created the world just like it says in the Bible."

"Right," he said. "And scientists who say the world is very old aren't just trying to lie about it. The rocks really do measure to be that old. But it may be that God created them old—like he did Adam."

I remembered the things I had learned about the Flood and *geology* (the study of rocks) before. "Or the Flood could have messed up the radiometric age of the rocks."

Radiometric dating is one of the ways scientists measure how old rocks are. Professor Bones looked surprised that I knew that. "Yes, that's right. Or God could have created the rocks of this world when he created the rest of the universe, then created this world during creation week like the Bible says."

He had to slow down as we came up behind a dirty pick-up truck pulling a cattle trailer. On the winding road, there was no place to pass.

"That must be one of the local ranchers moving some cows or sheep," the professor said. "Here, now we can pass." He pulled out and around. As we went by, I didn't see anything in the trailer. I waved at the driver as we passed the truck, but he just pulled his big cowboy hat down low over his face.

I gave up and looked back at Professor Bones. "Okay, so what does all that tell me about dinosaurs?" I asked.

"Remember that dinosaur bones are fossils," he said. "That means that minerals have replaced the cells of the bones. So the bones are now made of the same things that the rocks are."

I was way ahead of him. "So that makes the dinosaur bones as old as the rocks. And since the bones are inside the rocks, they had to be there when the rocks were formed. So dinosaur bones are measured to be millions of years old too."

"Okay," he said. "So what does the Bible tell us about dinosaurs? As much as it tells us about most animals on earth. Almost nothing. The Bible doesn't list all the animals created. At creation, when the world was perfect and people lived for hundreds of years, animals were probably bigger and stronger, too."

"So there could have been dinosaurs in the Garden of Eden?"

"Why not?" Professor Bones asked. "God must have created dinosaurs. And you have to remember that there were many different kinds of dinosaurs. Most of them would have been interesting to watch and probably fun to play with."

I tried to imagine Cain or Abel growing up outside the Garden of Eden, playing with a little stegosaurus or triceratops. That would be fun!

When we got back to camp, I told Kayla and Luis about it. "Did he say what happened to the dinosaurs?" Kayla asked.

"No." And I remembered something else. "He said the Bible might say a little about dinosaurs, but he didn't tell me what it says."

"Let's go find him," Luis said. On our way across camp, we saw Ranger Mahoney on her horse. We were going to stop and say hello, but she was talking to the people whose walkie-talkies were stolen.

"No, we don't have any more information," she told them as we walked by. "You know, in a town, the police usually know who the criminals are. So if something happens, they know who to question. But out here, there's no one around but campers who come and go every week."

"Is there a lot of crime out here?" the woman asked.

Ranger Mahoney laughed. "There used to be, back in the early days. This was a famous hiding spot for bank robbers and cattle rustlers. It's so far from everywhere that the outlaws could hide out with their stolen cattle for months."

I poked Kayla. "Maybe there's a famous outlaw in our camp. One of the Ten Most Wanted criminals."

She just rolled her eyes. The ranger was still talking.

"But these days? Why would there be? Oh, we have a few cases of vandalism—kids breaking things or painting the rocks. Sometimes, there will be a rash of stealing. But it doesn't last long. Usually, the thief is one of the campers and either we catch them and turn them over to the sheriff, or they pack up and leave before we can."

The man stared at us. "Well, I have a few ideas about who the thief is around here. Or thieves."

We kept walking.

Professor Bones wasn't around, and since it was starting to get dark, we headed back toward our tents. "Let's go by the teenagers' camp," I suggested. "I have an idea."

"Are you sure?" Kayla asked.

"Trust me," I said. "And go along with whatever I say."

The teenagers were out by their fire. I didn't look at them, but I talked loud enough for them to hear.

"Let's go down by the river where Mom and Dad are," I said to Kayla.

She stared at me. "Mom and Dad aren't—"

"I know," I interrupted her. "They told us to stay at the tent," I said, winking and tilting my head. She looked at me like I was out of my mind. "But nothing is going to happen to our little television. No one even knows we have one. We'll just leave it in the big tent."

I grabbed Kayla's arm and led her away quickly. Luis was right behind. "Did it work?" I asked him.

"Did what work?" Kayla asked, jerking away.

"They were watching and listening to you," Luis reported with a grin. "We'd better hurry back to your tent."

We turned to circle back around, but Kayla refused to move. She stomped her foot on the ground. "I'm not going anywhere until someone tells me what we're doing!"

"Kayla, it's a trap. I made sure they heard that there's a TV in our tent and that no one will be there for the next few minutes."

She started catching on. "So if they're the thieves, that's exactly where they will be headed. Come on! What are you guys waiting for? Let's go!"

Sisters.

Discoveries and Clues

Dinosaur Clues

Many scientists believe that life on earth evolved over millions and millions of years. Some believe that God started the process of evolution—some don't believe in God at all.

The rocks really do measure to be that old. But it may be that:

1. God created them old—like he did Adam.

2. The Flood could have messed up the radiometric age of the rocks.

3. God could have created the rocks of this world when he created the rest of the universe, then created this world during creation week like the Bible says.

If the dinosaur bones are inside the rocks, they had to be there when the rocks were formed. That's why dinosaur bones are measured to be millions of years old.

Words to Remember

Geology: The study of rocks

Radiometric dating: One of the ways scientists measure how old rocks are

Dinosaur Camp Mystery

This area used to be a hiding place for robbers, rustlers, and outlaws. Are there dangerous outlaws in camp?

If there are, we may have a way to trap them!

SIX

Footprints in the Canyon

Sizing Things Up

This morning started off in a very strange way. Of course, last night was kind of strange too. You won't believe what happened last night. Okay, maybe you will. We hid in the tent and waited to see if the teenage thieves would take the bait.

"It's a good thing Mom and Dad went on that walk," Kayla whispered. She was wrestling with a sleeping bag while Luis and I peeked through the tent flaps. "Do you see them?"

"Not yet," Luis answered. "Are you sure they'll come?" he asked me.

"I said that there was a TV in our big tent and that no one was there. If you were stealing stuff like walkie-talkies and cameras, wouldn't you try to grab a TV?" Luis nodded and kept watching.

"What do we do if they show up?" Kayla asked.

"They'll head straight into Mom and Dad's tent," I told her. "I wish we could see the front of the tent from here. Maybe we should wait until we hear them, then just sneak up and zip them in."

Luis shook his head. "Won't they just tear up the tent and get out anyway? I think we should run for an adult to help us."

"Too late," I hissed. "Here they come!" We watched as two of the teenagers walked slowly up the path right toward Mom and Dad's tent. "As soon as they're out of sight, we'll rush around to the tent door and shout as loud as we can. That should scare them off and bring some help."

We watched silently as they got closer. When they disappeared from sight, I led the way out of the tent. With Luis and Kayla right behind me, I dashed to our parents' tent, stuck my head in the open flap, and shouted as loud as I could.

"Gotcha!"

"Aaah!" The voice that screamed back didn't sound like an outlaw's. In fact, it sounded familiar.

"Zack!" Mom put her hand over her heart. "You scared me to death! What is wrong with you?"

"I, uh, well, I didn't know you were back," I stammered. I could hear Kayla and Luis laughing like I was telling jokes.

"And?" she said, tapping the ground with her toe, "you thought you'd exercise your lungs in my tent?"

"No, I thought someone else was in here." I tried to change the subject. "Where's Dad and Alex?"

"I left them visiting at Luis's parents' tent and came back to start supper. I think you just volunteered to help."

"Sure, Mom," I said as I backed away. Kayla was still laughing.

"I told you, Luis," she said. "Zack's traps never work right."

I didn't bother to correct her. I was watching our two suspects coming out of the camp restroom. And thinking up another plan.

This morning, I didn't even have time to swallow my orange juice before Luis ran into our camp. "Zack, someone else said they saw the dinosaur!"

He led the way down to the river where the early morning raft-riders were still dripping and pulling their · rafts out of the river.

"It was right up on the edge of the canyon," a man wearing an orange life jacket was saying. "I didn't get a good look. We were moving too fast. But whatever it was, it had a long skinny neck. And its head was twisting back and forth."

Buddy, the raft guide, laughed out loud. "What do you think it was, a giraffe? Come on, friend, you must have seen a tree or something."

The man shook his head stubbornly. "I know I saw something. Some kind of animal."

"Was it a dinosaur?" someone asked. The man didn't answer, but most people laughed and started walking away.

"Do you think he's crazy?" I asked Buddy.

He looked at me for a second, like he was thinking hard. Then he smiled. "You never know what's running around in these canyons."

"That settles it," I told Luis on the way back to camp. "We've got to go back to that canyon and figure out what's up there."

When I asked Dad if we could go exploring, he said, "Yes, but Professor Bones is taking us into town to see the Dinosaur Gardens. You won't want to miss that, so don't be gone long."

By the time Kayla, Luis, and I made it back near the top of the canyon, we were a little nervous. "What was that?" Kayla hissed as the leaves in a tree rustled. A small brown bird answered her question by flying away.

This time, we made it to the top without hearing that strange scuffling sound. "Keep your eyes open for clues," I said. "Whatever is up here should have left something behind."

"Ug," Kayla grunted as she backed away from a rock. "Some animal left something behind over there. But it doesn't smell like a clue."

"Hey," Luis called, "come look at this." He was kneeling by a patch of sandy dirt. "It's some kind of animal track."

"Wow! That's big," Kayla said. "What kind of animal would leave that?"

The print had three toes, with a claw mark at the end of each. Something about it seemed familiar. I tried to measure it. "It's bigger than my whole hand. It's bigger than both of my hands."

"It's a lot bigger than any bird tracks I've ever seen," Luis said. "You don't think … "

Kayla almost whispered, "It's not nearly as big as the dinosaur tracks we saw in Texas. But Professor Bones said that dinosaurs came in all sizes. Is it possible?"

I took a deep breath. "There's no way a real live dinosaur is running around up here. It has to be something else. Are there any more tracks?"

"Over here," Luis called. There was another print about fifteen feet away. We searched for more, but the ground was mostly covered with rocks and pebbles.

"We'd better go," I reminded them. "We can't miss the trip to the Dinosaur Gardens."

"What are we going to tell them about these tracks?" Kayla asked.

"Nothing," I said. "Let's figure it out for ourselves."

The first thing I saw in the Dinosaur Gardens was the head of a tyrannosaurus rex sticking up over the trees. Looking up at the six-inch teeth, I was glad that all the dinosaurs were dead.

"These statues are all life-size," Professor Bones announced to the group. "Most of them are based on the size of bones found at the quarry."

While Kayla played tag with Alex around the diplodocus's legs, I thought of a good question to ask. "Professor Bones, you said that the size of these statues is based on the size of the dinosaur bones. Is there a way to tell the size of dinosaurs by their footprints?"

"Well, the size of the footprint is certainly a clue," he said. "But length of the stride also tells you something."

I was confused. "The length of the stride?"

He showed me by taking a big step. "The length of a stride is the distance between your feet when you take a step. Since I'm about six feet tall, the length of my stride is about three feet. When paleontologists find dinosaur footprints, they measure how far apart they are. It helps them learn not only how big the creature was, but how they walked or ran—whether they used two feet or four."

I'm sure what he was saying was very interesting. But I didn't hear a word. All of a sudden, all I could see was those two big footprints above the canyon.

Fifteen feet apart.

SEVEN

Dinosaurs on the Ceiling

Or, Dinosaurs on the Roof

What?"

When I tried to tell Kayla and Luis what Professor Bones had said about dinosaur tracks, they didn't understand.

"What difference does it make that the two tracks we saw were *fifteen feet apart?*" Kayla asked.

"Look," I tried to explain, "if a person six feet tall leaves footprints three feet apart, how tall would someone be if they left footprints fifteen feet apart?"

Snap! "I get it!" Luis said. "Thirty feet tall!" Then his eyes got big. "Are you saying that whatever left those tracks above the canyon is," he pointed to the allosaurus nearby, "as tall as that? Thirty feet tall?"

Kayla looked up. For once, she was speechless.

"I'm not saying anything," I said. "Except this—let's

find out more about dinosaur footprints."

We found Professor Bones standing under an enormous apatosaurus. "This creature would have weighed more than thirty tons," he told the group around him.

"Tell us some more about dinosaur footprints," Kayla asked. I pulled out my notebook and pencil.

Professor Bones scratched his head. "You know that a dinosaur footprint is a fossil. It forms where a dinosaur stepped in a soft surface like sand or mud leaving a print. If that footprint is filled in by another layer of sand or mud, and the layers harden into rock, then a fossil is formed. The footprint becomes a part of the rock."

"That wouldn't happen very often, would it?" I asked. "After all, most footprints we make are washed away or wiped out."

"You're right, Zack. We don't find many footprints compared to the numbers of dinosaurs that must have been alive. But many dinosaur footprints have been found all over the world. There are hundreds in Massachusetts and Connecticut. The Paluxy River in Texas has uncovered huge footprints of a brachiosaurus."

"We saw those," Kayla said to everyone. "Everyone in our family stood inside one footprint!"

Professor Bones laughed. "The strangest kind of dinosaur footprints are the ones found underground—on the ceilings of coal mines."

"On the ceiling?" Luis threw up his hands. "How could dinosaurs walk on the ceilings of caves?"

I thought the professor was just trying to trick us. "We know that some dinosaurs could fly, but none of them could walk upside down."

The professor ducked like we might throw things. "I'm sorry, but it's true. But not in the way you think. The coal underground was formed when great chunks of *vegetation* were pressed down together and covered up."

"You mean like trees and grass and stuff?" Kayla asked.

He nodded. "Right. The large amounts of coal and oil found in this world is good evidence that at some point in the past, everything was turned upside down and buried."

"Like there was a worldwide flood or something," I muttered as I wrote in my notebook.

"But anyway, coal is often found in *veins*, long and skinny like the roots of a plant. Coal mines are long shafts dug along the coal vein. Basically, they dig the coal out and leave a tunnel between the rock layers."

"And dinosaurs walked around in these tunnels?" Luis still couldn't believe it.

"No," Professor Bones said, "they walked around

before the coal or rocks were formed. What miners find is the bottom side of the footprints."

"I get it," I said. "The dinosaurs walked around and squished down into the soft plant junk. Then the hole their footprint left filled up with mud. After it all got hard, the footprint was still there. Then the plant junk became coal and the miners took it out. That left the footprints hanging down from the ceiling like big bumps."

"Exactly!" Professor Bones smiled when he said it.

Snap! Luis got it too.

Dinosaurs' tracks in the ceiling of caves. Weird, huh?

"Professor," someone else asked, "what kind of dinosaur footprints are found around here?"

He shook his head. "Not really any in this area. That's one of the curious things about dinosaurs. We seldom find footprints and dinosaur bones together. It's as if they didn't live in the same area that they died."

"What do you mean?" Dad asked. He and Alex were listening too.

"Since we accept the Bible story of the Flood, it's easy for us to imagine that they left footprints as they tried to escape the waters. Or their bodies were carried away from where they lived."

"Did you get all that information?" Dad asked a little

later. "It seems like the kind of thing you could tell Bobby about."

I patted my backpack. "I got it all right here in my notebook."

While Professor Bones lectured to the adults, us kids wandered around the dinosaurs. Alex was with us, and he kept asking questions until I thought I was back in school.

"I don't know, Alex," I said. "I don't know why dinosaurs only had three toes. I don't know why T-rex couldn't just be friendly. I don't know why the triceratops had three horns. I just don't know!"

"Zack," he said, "even if the big dinosaurs wouldn't fit on the ark, why didn't the little ones get on? Why aren't there any live dinosaurs today?"

"Maybe there are," Kayla blurted out. Luis and I turned and glared at her. "Maybe, uh, maybe some small ones did. Like the crocodiles."

As soon as Alex was thinking about something else, I dragged her over by the stegosaurus. "What are you trying to do, scare him to death? Or convince everyone that we're crazy?"

"But what if he's right? What if some small dinosaurs did get on the ark, and are still alive?"

I banged my fist against the stegosaurus's stomach. "It's not a dinosaur. It can't be."

"Let's ask Professor Bones," she said. "He'll know for sure, won't he?"

"Okay," I said. "But let me ask."

After a while, we trapped the professor over by the allosaurus. I decided to find out a few things before I asked the really dumb question.

"Professor, you never really explained how to tell the size of a dinosaur by its footprints."

He nodded. "The footprints are an important clue. The larger the foot, the larger the animal, usually. And the deeper the print, the heavier the animal. But that's useful only if you know how soft the ground was when he stepped on it."

That didn't help. I had to try a different approach. Tapping the metal allosaurus on the leg, I said, "We talked about strides before. How big a stride would this allosaurus have? How far between its footprints?"

He tilted his head back to look over the statue. "Oh, about fifteen feet, I'd say."

Kayla's eyes got big. "What kind of dinosaur was this one? Shy, scared? A nice plant-eater?"

"Oh, no," he was quick to answer. "The allosaur, like the velociraptor, was a fierce hunter. In fact, along with those brachiosaur footprints in Texas, you can see the tracks of an allosaur. It's like he was following them."

We all turned to look at the enormous diplodocus statue. It was a smaller relative of the brachiosaur. "He couldn't have been hunting something that big—could he?"

"Oh, sure," Professor Bones said. "In fact, brachiosaur bones have been found with teeth marks still showing in them. And those teeth marks match with the allosaurus's teeth."

Suddenly, it seemed very important to know for certain whose tracks we had found above the canyon.

Discoveries and Clues

Dinosaur Clues

A dinosaur footprint is a fossil. It forms where a dinosaur stepped in a soft surface like sand or mud leaving a print. If that footprint is filled in by another layer of sand or mud, and the layers harden into rock, it makes a fossil.

Coal was formed when huge chunks of plants and trees were buried quickly. Dinosaur footprints in coal mines show that they were walking around in the mud when the Flood was starting to bury everything.

Dinosaur footprints are found in many places, but not often where dinosaur bones are found. It seems like they didn't live near where they died. Or else the Flood carried their bodies away.

The large amounts of coal and oil found in this world is good evidence that at some point in the past, everything was turned upside down and buried. Like in Noah's flood.

Words to Remember

Vegetation: Trees, plants, and grass

Veins: Long skinny sections of coal

Dinosaur Camp Mystery

We'd better find out for sure what's out there. And soon!

EIGHT

Strange Stones, Strange Moans

Echoes in the Dark

Two strange things happened today. The first one was kind of cool.

"When are we going to eat?" Alex called out. "I'm as hungry as a T-rex."

Professor Bones laughed. "Your brother's right. It is lunchtime. Let's break out the picnic."

While everyone was setting up paper plates on the picnic tables and digging out their sandwiches, Professor Bones kept talking to us. "You can see that many different kinds of dinosaurs were found in this area. But how do we know whether or not they really lived around here?"

"Well," I said, "you told us that there aren't any dino footprints around here. And that may mean that they didn't live in this area."

"Right," he said as he nodded. "But what about other clues? What do you think these dinosaurs ate?"

I looked around. Most of them were big plant-eaters. "Except for the T-rex and the allosaur, I think they all ate plants," I said.

He nodded again. "The big dinosaurs were all plant-eaters. That apatosaurus and that diplodocus had to eat tons of grass, reeds, or plant leaves every week. Now, you know that dinosaurs aren't the only kind of fossils we find, don't you?"

"I've seen pictures of fish fossils. And I have a fossil of a seashell at home," I said.

Professor Bones reached into his pack. "Here's a fossil of a leaf. You see, plants and grasses got caught in sand and mud, too. And sometimes they leave fossils, too."

I looked closely at the rock he handed us. You could see all the parts of the little leaf clearly.

"Did this come from around here?" I asked. "Is this what these dinosaurs ate?"

He shook his head. "No. And that's the problem. Very few plant fossils are found in the same rocks as these dinosaur bones. It seems that there were not enough plants here to feed these dinosaurs. So they couldn't have lived here."

"So what were they doing here?" Alex asked. "Were

they on vacation too?"

"No," Professor Bones answered with a laugh. "I think that either they were running away from the rising flood waters and got trapped here, or else they drowned wherever they lived and floated here."

I put down my sandwich and got out my notebook.

Alex stuffed his sandwich in his mouth. "I'm a T-rex. Roar!" he said around his food.

"Gross," Kayla muttered.

"Alex, chew your food," Mom said. "And don't talk while you do it."

The professor slid another rock down to me. It was smooth and shiny. "You might find this interesting," he said. "Do you know how chickens chew their food?"

"With their teeth?" Kayla said. Then she thought about it. "Wait, chickens don't have teeth."

Professor Bones laughed. "No, they don't. What they have is a gizzard. It's part of their digestive system. They eat tiny stones and the stones are trapped in their gizzard. Then when they eat seeds or grain, the stones help grind them up."

"So they chew with rocks in their gizzards." Kayla shook her head. "Chickens are weird."

"Well, not just chickens," he said. "It seems that some dinosaurs swallowed small stones too, to help them grind up the food they ate. Fossil skeletons have been found with a little heap of polished stones where the stomach of the dinosaur was. What you're holding, Zack, is a stone found in the the skeleton of a brachiosaur."

I looked at the stone again. "This was actually inside a dinosaur?"

He nodded. "It's called a *gastrolith*."

I was holding something that a dinosaur had picked up and swallowed. Is that amazing or what?

We stopped by a little store in town on our way back to camp. Buddy, the raft guide, was just coming out. "Hi," I said. "Taking a day off?"

"Why bother?" he answered. "There's nothing to do around here anyway."

"Did anyone see a dinosaur today?" I teased.

He didn't laugh. He just shook his head. "No. But we sure heard some strange sounds last night. Did you folks hear anything over at the campgrounds?"

"No." I thought maybe he was trying to tease me.

He never smiled. "Well, it didn't sound like a wolf or a coyote. I don't know what it was. But it sounded big."

I caught up with Mom and Dad near the bug spray. "You guys didn't hear any strange sounds last night, did you?"

"Just your brother snoring," Dad said. "Why?"

"Nothing, I guess. Dad, can I get a new flashlight? Mine is broken."

"Are you sure the batteries aren't dead?"

I nodded. "It went out when I swatted a mosquito."

He sighed. "Kind of an expensive flyswatter, don't you think? It sounds like you just broke the bulb. Maybe we can buy another one of those here."

We found the right bulb. "Let's get some more batteries, too," I suggested. "Just in case."

But they didn't have the double-A batteries we needed. When we checked out, Dad asked the clerk about it.

He laughed. "People have been asking for those all week. But we're out. Everyone in town is out. We missed a shipment. There won't be any more until next week."

Sheriff Tate was pulling in as we walked out. "How are you folks?" he asked. We stopped to talk. Dad told him about the stolen walkie-talkies.

He shook his head. "In the good old days, all they had to worry about was bank robbers and cow and sheep rustlers."

"I guess there's not much *rustling* these days," I said.

"No, not cattle or sheep," he said. "But we do worry about fossil rustlers. They try to steal valuable fossils. By the way, have you folks seen any trucks pulling trailers recently?"

I told him about the one Professor Bones and I had passed.

"Did you see the driver?" he asked. I shook my head. "Well, keep your eyes open. Thanks."

When we got back to camp, I discovered that I didn't need the batteries after all. Or the bulb.

Someone had stolen my flashlight.

"Are you sure you left it in your tent?" Mom asked as she helped me search through the sleeping bags again.

"I put it right under my pillow," I said. "There was no need to carry it around, since it didn't work. Why would anyone steal a flashlight that doesn't work?"

She shrugged. "Whoever took it just grabbed it and ran. They didn't take time to see if it worked. Then they probably threw it away as soon as they figured out that it was broken. Why don't you use mine for the rest of the trip? I'm not out exploring much anyway."

"Thanks, Mom."

It was just getting really dark when Kayla and Luis and I got back from the river's edge. We were trying to skip stones, but the fast current kept swallowing them up.

Then, from somewhere in the darkness, we heard it.

Hrroarrr! The sound echoed throughout the camp.

"What was that?" Kayla asked, moving closer to the

fire. No one answered.

Hrroarrr! The sound seemed to come from all around us.

"It doesn't sound like a coyote or bobcat," Mom said. "How far away do you think it is?"

"This must be the sound Buddy was talking about," I murmured. "Quiet, let's try to figure out where it's coming from." We listened closely.

Hrroarrr!

I pointed straight to the canyon we had explored. "It came from that way. Whatever it is must be up there at the top of that canyon."

"But what is it?" Dad questioned.

Alex shivered and wrapped his blanket tighter around him. "I know what it is," he said. "I've heard it before."

We all stared at him.

"It's on my dinosaur video. It's a T-rex hunting for his supper."

Discoveries and Clues

Dinosaur Clues

Very few plant fossils are found in the same rocks as these dinosaur bones. Since there weren't enough plants here to feed these dinosaurs, they couldn't have lived here.

Either they were running away from the rising flood waters and got trapped here or else they drowned wherever they lived and floated here.

Words to Remember

Gastroliths: Polished stones from a dinosaur's stomach

Rustling: Stealing cattle or sheep to sell somewhere else

Dinosaur Camp Mystery

My flashlight was stolen. Why would anyone take a flashlight that doesn't work?

Dinosaur Roar?

Trying to Put It All Together

*H*rroarrr!

It sounded farther away now. Mom didn't waste any time. "Alex, you know there are no dinosaurs alive today. Whatever it is, it can't be a T-rex."

"Right," Dad agreed. "We'll ask the ranger about it tomorrow. Now, Alex, it's about time for you to go to sleep."

Kayla and Luis and I scooted up closer to the fire. "Could it be a T-rex?" Kayla asked.

"No way," I snorted. "Think about it. The track we saw was big, but it wasn't big enough to be a T-rex. Besides, there are no live dinosaurs. And even if a dinosaur could be alive today, it couldn't live out here."

Hrroarrr!

The sound was even farther away. We listened for a while, but didn't hear it again.

"So it's not a T-rex. Then what is it?" Luis asked.

I couldn't say.

"Well, I'm not going back up there," Kayla said with a shiver.

The next morning, I woke up to the sound of car doors slamming. "What's happening?" I called out to Mom. She was drinking hot chocolate by the fire.

"It looks like some people are packing up to leave," she said. "I wonder why?"

I wondered too, so I went to find out. Kids can learn a lot just by hanging around, you know. Luis ran over to join me as Ranger Mahoney rode up on her horse.

"Good morning," she said as she dismounted. Luis offered to hold the reins, and she walked over to the campers who were packing. "Sorry to see you leaving so soon," she said.

"After last night, we can't leave fast enough," the man snapped.

Ranger Mahoney sighed. "Not more things stolen, I hope."

He stopped with an armful of sleeping bags and looked at her. "Didn't you hear anything last night?"

"Hear what?"

"That howling, roaring sound. Everyone's talking about it."

Ranger Mahoney looked puzzled. "We didn't hear

anything at the ranger station. What did it sound like?"

The man shrugged. "I've never heard anything like it. And people are saying it might have been a ... a dinosaur."

Ranger Mahoney looked like she was going to bust out laughing. But the man looked so serious, she couldn't. "That's impossible. Who's saying that?"

"Everyone. And we're getting out. Just in case." Then the man walked away with his sleeping bags.

Ranger Mahoney turned to us. "Well, did you guys hear this terrible sound last night?"

We nodded. "It did sound weird," I said. "My brother says it sounded like the T-rex on his dinosaur video. I guess a lot of people have seen that video."

She looked across the campground where two other campsites were being packed up. "But there aren't any dinosaurs," she murmured.

"Did you figure out who's stealing things yet?" I asked.

She shook her head slowly. "I don't have a clue."

I didn't bother to tell her about my flashlight.

Before long, we were all in the car following Professor Bones on another field trip. Luis got to ride with us, so we sat in the back with Kayla and tried to figure it all out.

"Let's look at the clues," I said. "We saw two big"

tracks in the sand. They had three toes like a bird, but whatever they were, they were bigger than a bird."

"A lady said she saw something up there," Kayla reminded us. "She saw a shadow against the canyon wall. It was big and it had a long neck, like a dinosaur."

"And a man saw something on the canyon wall while he was rafting the river," Luis added. "He said it had a long neck and a small head that was twisting back and forth."

I wrote it all down. "Then we heard the sound last night. It wasn't a wolf or mountain lion. It couldn't have been a T-rex. What could it have been?" I snapped my notebook shut. "We have to go back up there."

Before Kayla could say no, the van stopped. "Look at that," Mom said.

"How did they do that?" Dad asked.

"They must have been giants," Alex added.

We all climbed out and stared up at the funny-looking objects painted fifteen feet up on the side of a cliff wall. "Who painted that?" I asked.

Professor Bones arrived with the answer. "These paintings were done by the Fremont Indians who lived in this area around a thousand years ago. Indian paintings on rocks or cliffs or in caves are called *petroglyphs* (pet-trow-glifs)."

"How did they paint them so high off the ground?"

Kayla asked. "Were they that tall?"

"No, they were normal-sized people. But we don't know how they painted so far off the ground."

"It's not really painting, is it?" Dad asked. He was staring at the art with his binoculars. "It's kind of etched into the rock surface."

The professor agreed. "It's more carved in than painted on. We'll see a lot more petroglyphs when we get to Cañon Pintado."

"Where?" Kayla asked as we got back in the car.

"Cañon Pintado," Luis said again. "It's Spanish. It means 'Painted Canyon.' "

The next place we stopped wasn't a canyon. It was a cave!

"Welcome to Whispering Cave," Professor Bones said as we got out. "I thought you might like to see the inside of some rocks as well as the outside. This isn't a typical cave carved out by the water. It's really just a big crack in a big rock."

He reached into his car, but came out empty-handed. "I seem to have misplaced my flashlight. I'm sure I had it this morning. I put it in the glovebox along with my wallet. Now, only my wallet is there. How strange."

Someone handed him one of their extra flashlights and we were ready to go. Then Alex said, "Dinosaurs don't live in caves, do they?"

"Alex, dinosaurs don't live at all," Kayla announced. "Zack, you go in first."

Discoveries and Clues

Words to Remember

Petroglyph: A carving or inscription on rock

Dinosaur Camp Mystery

Two big tracks in the sand. They had three toes, but whatever they were, they were bigger than a bird.

Two people who say they saw something with a long neck like a dinosaur.

The sound last night. It wasn't a wolf or mountain lion. It couldn't have been a T-rex. What could it have been?

A Story in the Sand

Clues from the Past, Clues for the Present

I love caves, so I didn't mind being first. The crack in the rock was more than a hundred feet high, but it got narrower and narrower until finally even I couldn't go back any farther.

There were no dinosaurs inside.

I waited outside on the sand and thought about everything while the others finished exploring. By the time Kayla and Luis came out, I had an idea.

"Look at this," I said as I opened my notebook. "When we first got here, someone's radio was stolen. Then, a pair of walkie-talkies were gone."

"Then that lady's camera," Kayla remembered. "And your flashlight."

"And Professor Bones's flashlight today," I finished. "Why would someone steal just those things?"

Kayla shrugged. "Because that's what they could get their hands on?"

I shook my head.

Snap! Luis got it. "No. They could have grabbed the professor's wallet and they didn't."

"And when they grabbed the walkie-talkies, they left a pair of binoculars, remember?" I flipped through my pages. "And the lady at the quarry said the camera was taken out of her bag."

"Why didn't the thief just take the whole bag? Or her purse?" Kayla finished. "What kind of thieves are these?"

"Maybe they're just not very smart," Luis suggested. "It could still be those teenagers."

I wasn't convinced. "There must be something else. I just can't figure it out."

"Here I come!" someone shouted. Suddenly, Alex landed right between us. Sand flew all over.

"Alex!" Kayla jumped up and brushed the sand off. "Come on, I'll race you to the cars." They dashed off, kicking up more sand.

Professor Bones dropped down beside us as we coughed and fanned the dust away. "This sand reminds me of something," he said. "Have you guys ever tried to climb a sand dune?"

We both nodded. "I climbed a really big one at the

beach," Luis said. "Boy, was I tired when I reached the top."

"It's hard to climb when the sand slides out from under your feet," Professor Bones agreed. "And did you notice what kind of footprints you left behind?"

"Not really footprints at all," I answered. "Just big gashes in the sand."

Professor Bones settled back. "You might be interested to know that many dinosaur footprints have been found in sandstone. *Sandstone* is a rock layer formed from sand."

"So when the dinosaur walked on it and left its tracks, it was sand like this," I said.

He nodded. "And all over the southwestern United States, you can see dinosaur footprints in sandstone. And in most cases, the footprints are going uphill."

"So?"

He laughed. "I don't mean that the rocks are slanted up. I mean that the dinosaurs were walking uphill when they left the footprints. What's remarkable about that is that the footprints are sharp and clear."

Luis made a face. "If we can't walk uphill in sand and leave clear footprints, how can they?"

"That's what one paleontologist wanted to know. So he tried an experiment. He caught some salamanders and lizards and put them in a tank filled with sand. Then he watched. The tracks they left in the dry sand were not clear."

"That makes sense," I said.

Professor Bones went on. "So he filled the tank with enough water to cover the sand. This time, when the lizards walked uphill, their tracks were clear and easy to see."

I blinked. "So you think that when the dinosaurs left their tracks in the sand going uphill, the sand was covered with water."

He nodded. "Maybe they were going uphill to get away from the water. Maybe it was getting deeper all the time."

Snap! "Maybe it was Noah's flood!" Luis said.

Just then, Kayla landed beside us. Alex was right behind her. Since we were talking about sand and footprints, I looked at theirs. Something didn't look right. "Kayla, Alex, come here. Let me see your shoes."

"What is it, Zack?" Kayla asked.

"Look, Professor," I said. "Kayla's shoe is bigger than Alex's. But he left a larger footprint. Why?"

"Because he was running faster and he jumped harder," the professor answered. "When you run or jump, it adds more force to your step and makes your footprint larger."

Luis knew what I was thinking. "So if an animal was

running or jumping, its footprint might be larger than usual. Right?"

"Right," Professor Bones agreed. "And the footprints might be farther apart. That's why you need several footprints before you can tell much about the animal."

I nodded. Kayla nodded. "We definitely need to go back up that canyon," Luis whispered.

Farther along the road, we saw the sheriff's car parked off to one side. Dad pulled over and rolled his window down. "Problems, Sheriff?"

"No, no problem," he answered. "I'm just checking out some tire tracks. Have you folks seen any trucks or trailers today?"

"No, but we'll keep our eyes open," Dad answered.

I waved at the sheriff from my window. "Still chasing those rustlers?" I called.

He smiled. "I wish it was rustlers. They're more fun than this."

The camp was filled with shouting people when we got back. Most of them were in the campsite where the teenagers' tent was. That tent was being packed up in a hurry.

"I knew it was them," Luis said. "Someone must have finally caught them stealing."

We ran over there as soon as we got out. "What's

happening?" Luis asked someone. "Are they going to be arrested?"

"Arrested? Maybe they should be—for drinking. You can smell the beer on their breath. But they say they saw a whole herd of dinosaurs!"

Discoveries and Clues

Dinosaur Clues

All over the southwestern United States, you can see dinosaur footprints in sandstone. These clear, sharp footprints were left while the animal was walking or running uphill on a sandy slope.

This only seems to happen when sand is under water. So the dinosaurs must have been walking in water. Maybe they were trying to escape the rising water of the Flood.

Words to Remember

Sandstone: A rock layer formed from sand

Dinosaur Camp Mystery

List of things stolen:

- A radio
- A pair of walkie-talkies
- A camera
- Two flashlights

Why would someone steal a radio but not the binoculars next to it?

Why would someone steal a flashlight but not the wallet next to it?

Why would someone steal a camera out of a bag and not take a purse?

If an animal was running or jumping, its footprint might be larger than usual. So the animal that left the footprints we saw might not be as big as we thought.

=

ELEVEN

White-Water Danger

Suddenly It Hit Me!

The guy with the wild black hair spoke up. "We did see them! We were just hiking around up there, you know?" He pointed up toward the spot we had explored. "So we found this big flat rock in front of a little canyon and had a few beers. Then I climbed off and walked toward the canyon. All of a sudden, there was this awful shrieking attack cry!"

He wasn't making it up. I could see by the look on his face that something had scared him half to death.

"Then I could see them—hundreds of them!" he said with a wild look in his eyes. "Those long necks swinging around, those beady eyes staring at me. I turned and ran for my life!"

"I'll say he did." This came from a guy who was cramming the tent poles in the back of their truck. "We didn't catch up with him until he was halfway back."

Some people were laughing, some people were shaking their heads. "Aren't you going to report this to the ranger?" someone called.

"No way," black hair said. "We're leaving, man. And we're not coming back."

They were gone in five minutes.

The next morning, two other campers packed up and left. Mom got a little worried. "You don't think something dangerous is going on, do you?" she asked Dad.

"If you want to worry," he answered through a forkful of scrambled eggs, "worry about surviving the white-water rafting. That's the only dangerous thing going on around here today."

Dad's not exactly a water-friendly kind of person. In fact, the closer we got to the rafting place, the more nervous he sounded.

"I'm thinking," he said as we pulled into the parking lot, "maybe someone should stay on shore. Just in case, you know."

"You're going, dear," Mom said softly. "I'm not taking three children out on the river alone."

"Alex," he said, "maybe you and I should drive down and meet them when they get out of the rafts."

"No way," Alex said. "I want to go in the boats."

I guess Dad gave up hope after that.

After we got ready, us kids hung around by the river, waiting for the grown-ups. The rafts were piled up by a big rock nearby. "I wonder which one is ours," Kayla said.

"I hope it's this one," Luis answered. He moved up to pat a big yellow one. Before he even reached it, an alarm went off.

Whoop! Whoop! Whoop!

"What in the world is that?" Kayla shouted. She held her hands over her ears.

In a few seconds, Buddy ran out of the building and reached for a small black box sitting on the rock. "What're you kids doing down here?" he growled.

"We were just waiting for our raft ride," I said. "What's the alarm for?"

"To keep kids like you from stealing the rafts," he said. "It's a motion sensor. The alarm goes off when something comes too near."

"Don't worry," Luis said. "I think the thieves left last night."

"What?" Buddy was confused.

"Those teenagers in the camp," Luis explained. "They left last night."

"Oh," Buddy answered. Then, "Oh! Good!" with a big smile. "Maybe you should all leave. I hear it could be dangerous around that camp."

While he was walking away, he was talking to himself. "Kids. They should be inside the fence with collars on."

"He used to be nice. Remember?" Kayla said. "I hope he's not the guide on our raft. One minute he's smiley, the next he's grouchy."

Before long, someone was going over the safety procedures with us. "Be sure to keep your lifejackets on at all times. It won't be necessary to wear your helmets except through the rapids. If you do fall out of the raft, don't try to swim. Just let the lifejacket keep you floating and go feet-first downstream."

"Oh, great," Dad said softly.

"If you are close to the raft, someone will reach out to pull you in. If you are away from it, your guide will throw a line to you. Grab it and you'll be pulled back on board."

"I hope so," Dad mumbled.

"Okay, let's go," he called. As he stepped into the other raft, Buddy stepped into ours.

"You two guys are up front," he said from the back. Luis and I nodded. "Well, you'd better be hanging on tight. That's where the real action is. I'll get you there— you can count on that. You won't drown, but you might be scared to death."

"Lucky us," Kayla whispered from behind me.

The first part of our journey was quiet and peaceful. We floated through canyons with steep cliffs on both sides. Professor Bones pointed out something in the first turn.

"See that petroglyph? Right under it is an ancient Indian campsite. You can see where they built their fires."

Seeing those old Indian sites reminded me of a question I had. "Professor," I called from the front, "if people and dinosaurs lived at the same time, shouldn't there be fossils of them together?"

"Dinosaurs and people," Buddy snorted. "Even I know better than that." Then his expression changed. "Unless those sounds the other night were from real dinosaurs."

Professor Bones ignored him. "Zack, some people believe there are places where you can see dinosaur and human footprints in the same rock. But I'm not sure the marks they call human footprints are really that."

"Well, humans wouldn't leave as big a hole in the mud as a dinosaur would," Kayla said. "No wonder their footprints are hard to find."

"But other small animal footprints are found," the professor said. "It's really disappointing to find no fossil evidence of humans with dinosaurs. But maybe God didn't give us proof for a reason. Maybe he wants us to choose because we believe—in him and in the Bible."

"Why didn't the dinosaurs get on the ark?" Alex asked.

"Maybe some did," Professor Bones said. "Some of the smaller ones could have. But the new earth just didn't suit them, and they died off. God must have seen that since humans were becoming smaller and weaker, the big dinosaurs were just too powerful for humans to deal with—so he let them die."

By this time, we were a long way ahead of the other raft. I was watching when Buddy pulled out a big blue two-way radio and clicked it on. "Raft two, this is Raft one. Come in."

Nothing happened. He tried again.

"Raft Two, come in. Hey, Rick, are you back there?"

Still nothing. He shook it and mumbled under his breath.

Luis called my name. "Zack."

I ignored him. Buddy tried it one more time, then he said, "Batteries must be dead."

"Zack!" Luis said it louder. I waved him off. For some reason, I kept staring at Buddy as he opened the radio back and four batteries popped out.

All of a sudden, it hit me!

As I turned toward the front, a wave of white water hit me right in the face.

"Zack! Are you okay?"

I sputtered and spit for a second, but I was fine. "No problem," I said.

"That's what you think," Buddy called from the back. "Warm Springs Rapids—dead ahead!"

Discoveries and Clues

Dinosaur Clues

Some people think there are dinosaur and human footprints in the same rocks. It's not clear, though.

Maybe God wants to allow us to choose to believe the Bible story, instead of proving it.

God may not have allowed the big dinosaurs to survive because humans could no longer control them.

Dinosaur Camp Mystery

Those teenagers say they saw a whole herd of dinosaurs.

TWELVE

Batteries Not Included

The Pieces Start to Fall into Place

The water up ahead looked like waves coming in at the beach—only there was no safe sand to stand on. Our raft was floating like a bobber on a fishing pole line, just waiting for a big fish to snatch it under.

"Everyone hang on now," Buddy said, "and do what I tell you. When I say 'Now' everyone paddle as hard as you can."

He waited while we drifted closer to the foaming water. When we got next to a wave as high as my head, he shouted, "Now!" We paddled like crazy.

A wave buried Luis. "Are you still there?" I shouted when the water was gone.

"Yippee!" he shouted back.

Another wave rose up to my side. I ducked. "Aaah!" Kayla shouted when it crashed in her face.

Suddenly, the front of the raft dipped down. "Whoa!" I shouted as I tipped forward. I would have grabbed the side of the raft, but both hands were gripping the paddle.

The raft hit a wall of water and stopped. I kept going. I could see just where I was going to splatter against a big wet rock.

Then something yanked me back into the boat. I crashed back onto the seat and wedged my foot under the cushion. "You okay?" Dad shouted in my ear.

"Yeah!" I shouted back. "Thanks. And Dad, you can let go of my belt now."

A couple of bumps and splashes later, we were floating on smooth water. "I thought you were gone," Kayla said. "You bounced up like a rubber ball. Good thing Dad grabbed you."

"I'll say," I said. "Dad, I didn't think you would be so brave on the river."

"Brave?" He poked me with his paddle. "I just knew that if you fell in, your mom would make me go get you."

As we got close to the end of the trip, Professor Bones pointed ahead. "Down there is what they call Split Mountain. Usually, when a river bumps into a mountain, it goes around one side or the other. But this river went right through it."

"How did it do that?" I asked.

He shrugged. "No one really knows. Scientists don't really have a good explanation for it. Some might say that the river slowly ate its way through the mountain. But the easiest path for the water would be around the mountain."

"How do you explain it?"

He grinned. "I think a lot of geology is hard to figure out—unless you believe in Noah's flood."

The rafts landed right back in our campground. "That was great," Mom said to Buddy. "You must have fun doing that over and over all day."

He shrugged. "It's okay. The good part is, as soon as this raft is locked up, I have the rest of the day off. And I need to rest. It's gonna be a long night."

Kayla tilted her head and stared at him. "I thought he said that there's nothing to do around here at night."

"Grown-ups are strange," I said. It wasn't until we were nearly back to camp that I remembered. "Kayla, Luis, I figured it out."

"Figured what out?" Kayla asked.

"Why those things were stolen. The thieves weren't stealing radios or flashlights or cameras at all."

Kayla and Luis looked at each other. "Zack, are you sure you didn't hit that rock?" she asked.

I ignored her. "They were stealing batteries!"

Snap! "That's right! Everything that was stolen had

batteries—probably the same size batteries. That's what they needed. That's why they didn't take other things."

I nodded. "That's why they took my flashlight even though it didn't work. They just wanted my double-A batteries."

Kayla remembered something else. "Isn't that the kind the store was out of?"

"Right," I said. "But we still don't know who or why. Who needed double-A batteries so bad they were willing to steal them?"

No one had an answer for that.

Right after we ate everything in sight, we headed back up the canyon. "What do you think that teenager really saw up here?" Kayla asked.

"Who knows," Luis answered. "When my uncle used to drink a lot, he saw giant pink bunnies in his closet."

"Wait!" I hissed. "Did you hear that?"

We listened and I heard it again. It was that same shuffling, scraping sound. And it was coming from above us again. Kayla started breathing faster. "Either we run back to camp and never come back," I whispered, "or we run to the top and try to see what it is."

"Well," Kayla whispered back, "can we vote on it? Oh, all right, I'll follow you."

Pebbles started falling on us again as we raced for the

top. The closer we got, the slower we ran. Finally, I staggered up to level ground. Luis and Kayla were huffing right behind me.

"Look!" Luis wheezed. "There it is!"

We heard the scraping, shuffling sound again—as a marmot pushed rocks away from its burrow. They rolled down the slope.

"It must be digging a new burrow," I said, shaking my head. "Let's not tell anyone that a two-foot-long mountain rat chased us down the canyon last time, okay?"

"Is this the spot?" Kayla asked. We were looking for that footprint again.

"I think so," I said. "But all that's here now is two big old human footprints. It looks like those teenagers stomped all over our tracks,"

"So what do we do now?" Luis asked.

I shrugged. "I guess we track the wild teenagers. At least we can try to figure out where they were."

We followed their footprints and found the big flat rock in front of a small canyon. Kayla climbed up on top. "Yeah, this is the place," she reported, holding up an empty beer bottle.

"Hey, Zack," Luis called from behind the rock, "what's this?"

I found him looking at a little black box sitting on a

crevice in the rock. "I thought it was one of those motion alarms, like at the raft place," he said. "But it didn't go off when I came up close."

I picked it up. There were no markings on it at all. "Who knows?" I said, setting it back down. "What would a motion detector be doing up here anyway?"

Kayla leaned her head over the side above us. "What do you think?" she asked.

My stomach rumbled. "I think we head back," I said. "I don't want to be late for supper. Let's keep our eyes open for tracks as we go."

I had just taken my first bite of a great burrito when Mom pulled out a letter. "Hey, look what came to us at the ranger station," she said. "Ranger Mahoney dropped it off a few minutes ago."

I kept chewing.

"It's a letter from your Uncle Clint," she said.

My mouth froze. Suddenly, the last pieces fell into place and the puzzle made sense.

"Raz dag? Raz ratha mahoho!"

They all looked at me like I had sprouted horns. I swallowed and tried again.

"Where's Dad? Where's Ranger Mahoney?"

"Your father went into town. I think the ranger is somewhere here in camp. What's the emergency all of a sudden?"

I looked over at the setting sun. "I don't have time to explain, Mom. Kayla, find Ranger Mahoney. Tell her to meet me at the top of the canyon. And hurry."

She turned to run, but Mom's voice stopped her. "Hold it! No one moves until I know what's going on!"

"Mom, I think I can help the ranger find the people who've been stealing things. And maybe help the sheriff with his case too. But we have to hurry," I pleaded.

She wavered. "You won't go past the canyon with the ranger?" I nodded. "And you'll have her call the sheriff?" I nodded again. "Okay, but be careful."

"Thanks, Mom," I shouted over my shoulder. Then I turned. "Luis, come on!"

THIRTEEN

Dino-Surprise!

Things Aren't Always What They Appear

Luis and I barely had time to peer over the edge of the canyon before Kayla and the ranger rode up on her horse.

"Zack, what is this all about? Your sister made it sound like an emergency."

"It is," I told her. "There's something up here you're not going to believe unless you see it for yourself."

She shook her head. "Don't tell me you believe the stories about live dinosaurs up here."

Kayla chimed in. "Yeah, Zack. Don't tell us it's really dinosaurs."

I shook my head. "You wouldn't believe me. I almost don't believe it myself. Did you call the sheriff?"

She nodded. "I did, but I don't know why."

"Can you tell him to meet us up here?"

She did. Then she shook her head. "He thinks we're all crazy. Okay, Zack. Lead us to it."

When we got the horse parked, I led the way back

across the plateau toward the flat rock. "Everyone up on top," I whispered. "And keep quiet. I'll be back in a minute."

When I climbed up a few minutes later, Luis got restless. "Do you want me to go get that black box from the back side?" he asked. "We could show Ranger Mahoney."

"No!" I said sharply. "It is a motion detector, just like the one at the rafts. But this time, it'll go off."

"Why?" Luis asked. "It was dead this afternoon."

"Now it has a new battery," I said. "Shh! Here they come."

We could hear the truck better than we could see it without its lights on. But it was definitely a truck. And it was pulling a trailer. "What is a truck doing out here at night?" Ranger Mahoney wondered. "Let's go find out."

"Wait!" I said. "How far away is the sheriff?"

She radioed him quietly. "Just a few minutes. I told him to keep his lights off too. Are we ready yet?"

"Just another minute or two," I said. We waited, then we heard both truck doors open and close. "Two of them," I muttered. "We can't wait any longer. Are you ready? Watch this."

"How?" Kayla muttered.

"Turn on your flashlights," I said. Then I rolled a rock off the slope.

Whoop! Whoop! Whoop!

In the quiet darkness, the alarm sounded like an explosion. I aimed my light into the canyon. Suddenly, another explosion started there. Dozens of long necks popped up and long legs started running.

Running right at the two people from the truck.

"Hey," one of them shouted, "what's going on? Look out!"

With everyone's flashlight on the moving creatures, it was easy to see what they were.

"Emus!" Kayla shouted. "What are emus doing here?"

"Emus!" Luis shouted. "What are emus?"

Ranger Mahoney was speechless.

The two men disappeared in a sea of running birds. Suddenly, the lights of the sheriff's car came on behind the truck, and the big birds ran back toward the canyon. I reached down and grabbed the alarm and yanked the batteries out.

The quiet was broken only by the sound of the emus calling to each other. Then Sheriff Tate's voice rang out. "And just who do we have here?" he said as he yanked one man back on his feet. "Buddy! I might have known you would be involved in this."

"Zack, are you there?" It was Dad's voice. We all climbed down to meet him.

"Just a minute, Dad," I called. I ran over to the canyon and opened up another box by the canyon wall. "If I put the batteries back in the fence control, the emus will stay inside."

While the sheriff locked Buddy and his friend in his car, Ranger Mahoney had a question. "Zack, how did you know there were emus up here?"

I shook my head. "I should have figured it out sooner. My uncle has an emu ranch in Texas and we were just there last week. But that first footprint we saw was so big! And with all the dinosaur talk, I just didn't place it until tonight when we got that letter from Uncle Clint."

Dad laughed out loud. "I want to hear the rest of this, but let's get back to camp. Your mother will be worried sick."

Sheriff Tate walked up behind. "I want to hear that story, too. Let me call in a deputy to take those two in and see to these birds, and I'll join you." He shook his head. "Emu rustlers—who would have believed it."

FOURTEEN

Some of God's Favorites

Goodbye Dinosaur Camp

It's hard to believe we're almost halfway home. It seems like I just said goodbye to Luis and Professor Bones.

What a lot of excitement there was that last day at Dinosaur Camp! At the campfire with my hands wrapped around a cup of hot chocolate, I told the whole story.

"I finally figured out today what was really being stolen from the campers. It was the batteries. But I couldn't figure out who would need all the batteries."

Dad remembered. "The store was out of those batteries. In fact, the clerk said there wasn't one in the whole town."

"That's why Buddy began stealing them," I added.

Ranger Mahoney nodded. "He always seemed to be around when something was missing."

"Remember what he said about kids, Kayla?" I asked. "He said that they should all be fenced in and collared. I thought about little Winston, the dog next door. His yard has an underground fence and his collar shocks him if he goes past it."

"And the motion detector alarm at the raft place didn't have any wires leading to it," Luis added. "It ran on batteries."

"Just like the one out at the flat rock," I said. "When I figured out that they were the same, I felt sure they had a battery powered underground fence too."

"That's why the emus had collars on," Dad said. "No wonder they needed so many batteries."

"So that's what the woman saw that morning in the canyon," I said. "One of the emus must have gotten out, and she saw the shadow of that long neck."

"And the guy in the raft, too. He saw an emu up on the canyon wall," Ranger Mahoney decided. "He just didn't know what it was."

"I guess those teenagers weren't so drunk after all," Luis's mom added. "They must have set off the alarm and thought it was a dinosaur hunting call. And then all those emus popped up—no wonder they ran!"

"Then what was that other sound the other night?" Mom asked.

"I can answer that," Sheriff Tate said. "Buddy confessed that after he heard people talking about real dinosaurs, he thought he could scare everyone away. So he tape recorded a dinosaur roar from a TV show. Then he played it over the speakers of his truck. With all the echoes around here, it sounded real."

"What were they doing with the emus, Sheriff?" I asked.

He laughed. "They really were emu rustlers. Buddy got into it to make some quick money. These emus were stolen in Texas and were supposed to be sold up in Idaho. They'd been hiding the birds here until they could take them across the state borders safely."

"Using underground fences made them hard to spot in these canyons," Dad said.

Sheriff Tate agreed. "I guess it always has been a good place for rustlers to hide."

On the last day of Dinosaur Camp, Professor Bones had to tell everyone about the emus and they all had a good laugh. "The sheriff tells me that Buddy threw all the stolen items into the river," he reported. "So I guess we won't get those things back. But I hope we all take something about dinosaurs with us when we leave. Not bones or fossils, but a better understanding of how these wonderful creatures were a part of God's creation."

When we were packed up and ready to go, he stopped to say goodbye. "Thanks for coming, folks. And thanks for asking so many questions." He smiled at Kayla and me.

"There's one question you never answered," I said, opening my notebook. "You told us that the Bible might mention dinosaurs. But you never told us where."

"Okay," he said with a laugh, "one last answer. The book of Job is one of the oldest in the Bible. Some people believe it was written even before the book of Genesis was. It could be about times before Noah's flood. In Job 40, God is talking to Job about how he created the world. In verses 13 to 24, he talks about a creature called *behemoth* (buh-he-muth)."

"Behe-what?" I asked.

"It's just a word that means an enormous creature," he explained. "Some people think this was a hippopotamus or an elephant. But I think it describes a dinosaur—maybe even a brachiosaur. It's stronger and more powerful than any creature, but it hides under the water plants. Read about it sometime."

I wrote that down.

"And," he went on, "all of Job 41 is about an amazing sea creature called *leviathan* (lev-eye-uh-thon). Read about it—that's truly a remarkable animal. But my favorite part is in Job 40:19. It says that these creatures rank among the first works of God. If God thought that much of them, I'm glad I can study and find out more about them."

Now we're already out of Colorado and I'm still writing in my notebook. I got Luis's address so I can write and keep in touch with him.

I learned a lot I can tell Bobby about dinosaurs. They fit into the Bible story just fine. Sure, you can take millions of years to explain them. Or you can choose to believe the Bible.

I can't wait to tell him all about it. Especially the part about the emus.

Discoveries and Clues

Dinosaur Clues

My Conclusion: Now I think about dinosaurs as part of God's wonderful creation. If those verses in Job are really about dinosaurs, then God must have really enjoyed them. I like that idea, because now I think God will want dinosaurs in heaven. I know I do!

Danger at Dinosaur Camp

Spiritual Building Block: Courage
Learn more about true courage and how it can help you face your fears.

Think About It:

In the teaching camp where Zack and his family are learning about dinosaurs, there have been sightings of strange creatures, weird nighttime noises, and a rash of thefts. Many families departed the camp when the ranger and the sherriff could offer no explanation for all those mysterious events. How would you react under those circumstances? Think about a time when you were scared. What did you do?

Talk About It:

Talk to your parents, your church youth leader, or a trusted adult about a time when they were scared. What did they do? Ask them if they would do anything differently today, and why? What has changed?

Try It:

Read the story about Joshua and Caleb in the Bible (Numbers 13: 16-33). They encountered giants, huge armies of people, and many natural barriers that seemed to make it impossible for the Israelites to possess the land. All the other scouts brought back a discouraging report. But Joshua and Caleb told the people that the land was good and they could certainly take possession of it with God on their side. Like Joshua and Caleb, Zack showed courage by facing his fears. How can you do that in your everyday life? What could happen if you do face those fears? What could happen if you don't face your fears? God promises to be with us in everything we do. Thank him for helping you when you are afraid.

Detective Zack:
Secret of Noah's Flood

"Nobody believes Noah and his flood is a true story!" At least that's what Zack's friend Bobby says. What do you believe? Discover the truth about Noah's flood in this action-packed story that will capture your imagination while it builds your faith in the Bible.

ISBN: 0-78143-730-X....................Retail Price: $5.99

Detective Zack:
Mystery at Thunder Mountain

A "tribe" of unbelievers, strange cries in the night, large footprints in the canyon, and a series of thefts have Zack and Kayla searching for answers at Thunder Mountain Camp. Who is taking the horses out of the corral at night, and why? The list of suspects is growing longer every day. Everything is not what it seems at this summer camp.

ISBN: 0-78143-731-8....................Retail Price: $5.99

Coming Soon!

Detective Zack: Secrets in the Sand
Detective Zack: Red Hat Mystery
Detective Zack: Missing Manger Mystery